Wide Awake
Volume VII

Ukiyoto Publishing

All global publishing rights are held by

Ukiyoto Publishing

Published in 2022

Content Copyright © Ukiyoto

ISBN 9789367954874

All rights reserved.
No part of this publication may be reproduced, transmitted, or stored in a retrieval system, in any form by any means, electronic, mechanical, photocopying, recording or otherwise, without the prior permission of the publisher.

The moral rights of the author have been asserted.

This is a work of fiction. Names, characters, businesses, places, events, locales, and incidents are either the products of the author's imagination or used in a fictitious manner. Any resemblance to actual persons, living or dead, or actual events is purely coincidental.

This book is sold subject to the condition that it shall not by way of trade or otherwise, be lent, resold, hired out or otherwise circulated, without the publisher's prior consent, in any form of binding or cover other than that in which it is published.

*"Be fearless.
Be a lion.
Be like lava.
Rip them apart,
and burn their bones.*

*And when you are done,
tell the world that
you belong to no man.
That you are a lady,
a warrior,
a tsunami,
and you belong only to yourself."*

— Zaeema J. Hussain, The Sky Is Purple

CONTENTS

Short Story By Khrystine Soldao	1
Short Story by Isha Chopra	13
Poem by Piyali Mitra	17
Short Story by Sudakshina Bhatta	20
Poem by Narita Ahuja	31
Short Story by Dr. Barnali Das	38
Poem by Bhawna Mishra	42
Short Story by Debanjali Nag	45
About the Authors	*55*

Short Story By Khrystine Soldao

Reflect

"How about you, Doc. Did you experience bullying because of your appearance?" One of the attendees asked me.

I was invited in this seminar to be one of the speakers to advocate women empowerment.

I gave them a smile before shook my head, "I didn't get bullied because of my appearance but because of my attitude and background." Confusion became visible in their face so I continue, "I was once a bully too."

"How? What happen, then?" they asked in synch.

And I started reminiscent my war freak era.

"What the hell?!" I exclaimed when a girl suddenly bumped me. And I became more pissed to her look, a four-eyed stupid girl. I arched my brow when she looked at me straight in the eyes.

"I'm sorry but you're also at fault here, you're oblivious with your step," she stated calmly.

I laughed without humor and pushed her violently. "Damn it, I hate your guts! Did you see your dirt spot in your face duh you're not even pretty. And seriously, do you think that you're sexy? C'mon fatty, wake up! You should justify your confident to your face." I was about to grab her hair when my boyfriend suddenly came and dragged me away from her.

As we entered inside the vacant classroom, I released my wrist from his grip and glared at him. "Why did you do that? I'm not yet done with her!"

"C'mon, you're making a scene on the hallway. And professors might see you if I didn't do that." He heaved a sigh and gave me a peck, "Chill out, 'kay?"

Out of annoyance, I attacked his lips and heat starts to fire.

I chuckled after sharing that scene to them, "Yes, I agree that I'm really childish that time. But it was one of the memorable parts of my life."

"Why, Doc? Because is that your first-time making out?" the blonde lady asked.

I can't help but to laugh to her question, "No, no, that's not the first time I've done that with him." I cleared my throat and smiled at her, "It was because I met that girl, it was the first time I met my angel."

"Babe, I'm pregnant." My voice cracks. Trying hard to be brave in front of him.

He gasped and looked at me in disbelief, "You're kidding me, right? Stop it babe, that's not a good joke."

"Douchebag, this is not a joke."

"Tell me, that's not mine, right?"

I laughed in disbelief, "What the hell, are you shitting me right now?!"

"Why, I'm not even sure if that's really mine. You're a porn star!"

"I was! But you know that I stopped when we're together, so don't give me that shit!"

"Damn it!" He messed up his hair and kicked the chair near him, out of rage. He let out a deep sigh and looked at me straight. When he shook his head, I already know the answer. I sarcastically smiled at him and nodded as I give up. "I'm done with this. Let's just break up. I won't accept that so the decision it's all up to you. Abort or not, I'm out." And he turned his back on me. Tears starts streaming down my face when I left alone here on the rooftop. Pain blind my mind. And I've just found myself standing at the edge of this rooftop. Ready to bid my farewell to the world when someone suddenly spoke behind me. "Do that and ready to be a murderer."

I turned on her, and it was a girl last time. "What, murderer?!"

She smirked and nodded, "I accidentally heard your conversation with your boyfriend. You're pregnant so if you jump, you didn't just kill yourself but also the child in your womb." I swallowed hard as I realized what she's trying to say and glanced at my tummy. "So, what, murderer?" she mocked me.

I glared at her and decided to go down. "Fuck you, I'm not a murderer!" I shouted and walked out.

As I got home, I was greeted by clamor from my parents' quarrel. "Let's file a divorce! I'm so tired of you and your affairs," Dad said while carrying a bag and suitcase. Ready to leave our home.

"If that's really what you want, then sure! Leave and never show up again!" Mom even pointed the door. And Dad finally left.

"Mom?!" I called and she turned on me with shock in her face. "This is absurd! Divorce? Affairs? Oh my god, what have you done?" I cried out.

She just shook her head and go upstairs. She soon came down with carrying a bag and suitcase. She even gave me a sad smile before going out the door. I tried to ran after her but I saw her fetching by a man inside the gray car.

I was left dumbfounded. Wow how funny my life is, everybody just left me in a day! My tears instantly flowed down as I caressed my tummy. "You're the only one I have, so please don't ever leave me baby."

"Did you hear? Her parents got divorced." A group of people gossiping me.

I heaved a sigh, trying hard not to be affected by them. I decided to drop out so I'm here right now on campus. My parents are kinda popular here. Dad is a chancellor while Mom is one of the professors here. One of the reasons why I wanted to drop out since they're related in this school. And I hate the fact that my reputation here are utterly damage. And everybody is now starting to look down on me.

"There's also a rumor that her boyfriend dumped him."

"Oh really, why?"

"They say she got pregnant with other man."

"Dang, a disgrace girl!"

"You know, she deserved it. She's too confident on her image plus her nasty attitude."

"I agree. She wasted her pretty face just to flirt."

"Shame girl."

Their words pang straight on my chest. I was about to breakdown in front of them when I suddenly dragged by someone. "Girl, what the hell are you thinking?"

She asked irritably and handed me a handkerchief. "Jeez wiped your tears please, it's annoying!"

I wiped my face using the handkerchief she gave. A moment of silent between us until I spoke, "Why?" Her forehead creased so I continued, "Why did you help me?"

She rolled her eyes, "Duh, don't assume anything. I didn't help you. I just hate seeing a pathetic image."

"Still, thank you," I just said.

And she looked at me with surprise was visible in her face. She covered her mouth in disbelief, "Omg! Did you just said thank you?" I smiled melancholy at her. "Holy cow, I didn't expect that I will hear a thank you from you."

I chuckled a bit, "Yea, I didn't expect myself too, asking for your forgiveness." She remained silent and I heaved a sigh. "I'm sorry about our first encounter," I sincerely said.

"Wow, is that really you?"

"Yeah, I'm real."

She suddenly flicked her fingers. "Oh, snap! I was really fed up that day because of you but yea let's just forget it. I don't wanna add on, on your fucked up situation." My heart melts because of her words. "Really, thank you. You already helped me twice. I owe you big time!"

"Damn it, stop the drama," she grimaced.

I laughed and shrugged, "Okay, can I hug you instead?" At first, she hesitates but allow me eventually. I unfold my arm and embraced her. "You have no idea how much your presence succors me."

Her chest heaved and tapped my back, "C'mon, everything's going to be fine. Just believe in yourself, you can get through with it. You will be happy again."
I don't know but I started to get emotional with her words. I leaned on her shoulder as my tears flowed down. "I don't know. I'm really scared, really scared for my baby. I don't know if I can manage to raise him alone. I'm really wrecked in my situation right now. My family, my lover, and my reputation are already ruined. Damn it, I badly want to disappear! But this baby, this baby is the only reason why I'm still breathing right now. But I'm afraid if, what if he'll hate me as his mother? Fuck, I'm really ashamed to myself. They're right, I deserved all of this! I am a terrible person!"

"Shh, stop thinking that way. You're not a terrible person. You're just one of those people who are unaware by what they're doing so they made a mistake. So, don't let yourself to be affected by their words because first and foremost nobody deserves to be in ill-fated situation. Just trust yourself and keep going. Don't waste your precious life by being ashamed of who you are. Know your worth and used it as your motivation to be tough. C'mon, think this a lesson not a karma for yourself. Learn from this experience."

I let go of the hug and dry my wet face. My eyes and nose are already puffy. "Ghad! Can we, uh I know I have a thick face! So, can we be friends?" I asked with a husky voice due to crying.

"Hays, what a nuisance! Even you've cried foolishly, your beauty hasn't diminished. Unfair! How about me?" she joked.

I chuckled, "I know right, you're pretty too."
She rolled her eyes. "Inside, just pretty inside. Don't fool me, girl! That's not what you said to me last time." She laughed awkwardly when she noticed my silence because her remarked. "C'mon, I was just fooling around you know! I'm already cool to the words you said last time. Even tho, I'm ugly outside but I'm still confident for my imperfections. But let me tell you this, body shaming is not really nice. Downgrading women because of their size and appearance are idiotic. You don't know this, but having flaws isn't easy, it was never easy for us to build a self-esteem to face others with our own defects. It's just that, so next time try to prevent yourself from insulting someone."
"Don't worry, there will be no next time. From this day on, cross my heart I will no longer do that. I will be like you instead." I gave her a genuine smile.
She raised her brow, "Like me?"
"Like you, a right-minded and a kindhearted person," I casually said.
She scowled, "Jeez, stop that. Stop fluttering me and just fix your filthy attitude."
I acted hurting, "Harsh."
"But true," she added and we both laughed.
I held out my hand, "I'm Divine."
"Angel." And she reached out my hand.
"And that's where are friendship began. She's been my companion afterwards. She also helped me with my pregnancy. And I started to believe since then that sometimes you have to lose something to gain something better. My parents left me as well as my

boyfriend, but I'm fortunate enough that a baby and a friend suddenly came to save my life and to be the reason of my life changing."

Silence prevailed after I told my story. Someone suddenly raised a hand and I gave her a nod as permission to speak. "Uh I'm just curious. Doc, did you two still communicate? And how old your child is right now?"

I let out a deep sigh and began to speak.

"Where's my baby?" I instantly asked as I woke up after my cesarian delivery.

"Your baby was delivered successfully. The baby is premature so it's inevitable for him to suffer from respiratory distress syndrome," Doc said.

I'm became worried. "Where is him, Doc? I wanna see him right now."

"Nurse will assist you to NICU." Doc signals the nurse before walked away.

Tears flowed down as soon as I saw my poor baby intubated. The pain is killing me because of the thought that I wouldn't able to lift my own child. A sudden anxious I felt when nurses and doctor approached my baby in rush.

"Time of death, 7:25 am." I wept when the doctor called it.

I cremated my baby. I still can't accept, it's hard to accept that he's gone as well. And I don't know where Angel is right now. I haven't seen her yet since I woke up. I just discharged, and now I'm packing my things. While organizing my things, I saw an envelope. I

stopped from what I was doing and get the envelope. I sat on the bed and opened it as I saw it was for me.
I read the letter and tears starts running down on my face.

My friend Divine,

Hi, how are you? I left this letter with your things before I sent you to the hospital. I'd stay with you when you successfully delivered your baby boy. And I was also the one who first hears the news about your baby. So, what happen? I'm sorry if I was not there with you. I'm sorry if I just left you this letter as my farewell.

I will undergo surgery. A heart transplants. My doctor said that there's a chance my body will give up in the operating table. But still, I take the risks. I hate promises so please don't wait me. If ever I woke up after, I'll look for you instead. But if after a month I didn't show, just conclude I really became an angel. Remember what I've said? Keep going whatever it takes. Don't worry, I'm always here to support and guide you. I love you.

PS: I'll take care of your baby here from above. So, don't worry. Just fulfill your promise to me, be the voice and an example of strong woman.

Your friend,

Angel.

"How, doc? How did you handle it all?" she asked while teary eyed.

Her question makes me teary. I cleared my throat, "Everything happens for a reason, it will either lessons or blessings. Lessons, I learned a lot from the pain and the experienced I go through. And blessings, because despite of what happened I'm here standing in front all of you. Empowering you as women, to become strong physically and mentally. Not just a doctor of mental health but your co-women, allow me to advocate our self-worth, our rights as women. You already heard my story. I was a porn star back then. I'm not proud of it but I'm not ashamed of it either. Why would I be ashamed by doing it, if I'm not doing an illegal? But yea, as you see, my boyfriend didn't accept my baby because of the fact that I was used to be a porn star. He judges and left me because of that. And people say I'm a flirt, bitch, disgraceful, they call me names. Yes, I used to be affected by them. Imagine, I was one a bully turned into a victim of myself in just a second. And my parents left me as well, maybe because I'm not a good daughter?" I joked. "What I'm trying to say is, learn from me, used my story as an example to know what's wrong and right. Back then, I'm really blind. I was downgrading women based on their appearances, just because I'm beautiful and I feel like I have a right insulting their ugliness. But when my friend slapped me by her words, I suddenly awaken from the realization. I talked as if I'm perfect but I have so many flaws too. The imperfection doesn't just define the image outside but also the inside. And this scar." I lifted the hem of my shirt to show them the scar I received when I delivered my baby. "This is the mark that my baby gave me. This mark tells my self-worth. Despite of what I've done, I realize that I'm still worth it as a mother, I'm still worth it to be a good woman. Everyone, always believe that you're a woman who deserves to be treated as woman. Your self-worth is only determined by you not by everyone else. And our rights will determine not just by law but also on how you value yourself. Women empowerment doesn't only exist when it's time to go against men, because women empowerment will also reflect on how we accept ourselves and how we respect each other. As women, don't let your own beliefs be ruined because of the people around you. Stand and fight for your worth and rights. Be wide awake!" Cheers and sound of claps started to booming around when I dropped my mic and bowed at them.

I stroke the bottle pendant of my necklace with my baby ashes inside. And glanced at the heaven. "Both of you will always be the reflection of my success."

Short Story by Isha Chopra

Don't Judge the Book by its Cover

Heard melodies are sweet but unheard melodies are sweeter. Everything seems greener on the other side. By looking into one's life never told about their in-depth injuries. I'm sharing a story of a girl, who's life seems greener but in actual it's empty. God created a Beautiful creation which turned out to be a beautiful person I.e. a beauty with brain. A beautiful girl, who is simple, intelligent, enthusiastic, eager to achieve something in life. God gifted her everything like beautiful of appearance along with beauty of soul. She is quite good at studies. She is from a below poverty line family. She has to do household chores along with studies. She saw television from the window of her neighbour's house. One day her loving father died at an early age due to conspiracy of her relatives, which turned out to be the biggest drawback in her life. She was in sixth standard , when she loses her father. This leads to biggest financial problem in her life. Her big brother sold his books to get the things done for her father's last journey. After that, her mother has to do household chores in other's house to earn for the living. They are five siblings in which two are boys and three are girls. The elder son tried to help her mother by doing some labor work. These struggles turned out to be the biggest trouble in her life. Later on, she was accused by her teacher for having makeup on her face which is real beauty or teenage hormones turned to be more active . But her teacher slept her in order to prove herself right. Later on, she was in class 10th , her tuition teacher proposed her to be get married. When she rejected, then he curses her. Later on, the curse of teacher has taken effect , she was not able to give her board exams. She got married to a person sic years older than her. She is just 16 years old when she got married. At the age of 17 years , she got pregnant with a baby girl. But due to bad circumstances she has to get back to her mom's house. Her husband got vanished, leaving her in pregnancy at the hospital, that was the first child of the couple. Don't know why society pressures the girl to get married to someone at an early age when she didn't knew what is right or wrong, or how to live with husband. God knows why such things happen. Here, again it's a conspiracy in her husband's family. They thought that she is beautiful, she will control her husband. God please help these nuisance creatures. After that she faced lots of problems in her life. She has 3 children along with many difficulties. She has lots of restrictions. She faced so much in her life because in her husband's life , he doesn't have a mother I.e from childhood he never saw his mother. So, there's no one to make him understand how to treat a woman I.e. his wife. He got all the bad upbringing from his maternal side, who didn't give the right values to him. They didn't even love their father. Some mistakes and misunderstandings can never be undo or changed. At the face of her children, she has to live a life full of struggles ,still no peace. She has broken a lot from inside but never shows on her face.

By looking at her, who will say that she is a same person who wants to do something in life , who loves studying, dancing , singing and a "chaat " lover specially "golgappe", who is a cheerful person. Some stories are meant to be unheard until someone wants to hear them from the bottom of their heart. She is still fighting with her life, because she loves her children. They are her life or means a world to her.

Moral:

It is easy to make or create a gentleman out of an ill-mannered child then to repair broken elders.

That's why we say, "Appearances are deceptive."

That is, no one knows the weight of another's burden.

Poem by Piyali Mitra

A Tribute to the Nightingale of India

Songbirds listening—
Her voice, as fresh as ever.
A mellifluous singer
The one who began singing
At the tender thirteen
Admired by people of many generations
Her songs could melt
Even the hearts of rock.

But somehow failed to impress
Some of the present era super 'eggheads'
The ones who pose question even to the euphonious
The voice of Mother Saraswati's
Favorite child is like a
Perpetual stream with full of tranquility.

The sweet sounds emitting
From the mouth of 'The Nightingale of India'
Are like rhyming superlatives
Dipped in maple syrups and
Not purple prose glaze as some observes.

She weaves magic when she
Retorts in a musical notation to the
Call of love even from a faraway land
(Aap Kahe Aur Hum Na Aaye)

Her honeyed voice and mystic tune
Together hand in hand
Lead us to the finest key
To any locked heart.

Her darting voice that traversed
Every alley to the chambers of heart
Is like a therapy that
We may need when we feel blue.

The prologue (alap)
Escaping her lips is like a
Ensorcelled butterflies
That radiate love lit lavender light
Upon that astral parcel
Lulling many a sapped and knackered eye.

Her mortal form has now been
Spiritual away to Eden
Though her existence may become
Nirvanic transcendence
She, however lives in our heart
And rules our thought with her voice.

Short Story by Sudakshina Bhatta

The Awaited Enlightenment

"Meera look, this is the school your father-in-law studied in," Sarla pointed towards the ancient red building. "*Sasurji* went to school? Prabhat never told me that *sasurji* was literate. I saw him using *angutha* on documents." The 29-year-old widow of Prabhat asked in awe.

"Meera, you must know how to show respect to your late elders. Just because you've appeared for your 12th exams, don't mistake yourself to be a *pandit*. Prabhat's *baoji* attended school but he had to leave his studies after a while. They belonged to a farmer's family, schooling was a luxury for them. Why would they waste money on education when all they need is a steady income? Education never feeds you, farming does" replied Sarla. "No *amma*, you're wrong, if they had pursued education instead of farming, today we would….. *Amma* beware of that dog, he's been biting everyone around."

"Everyone? Who is everyone?" Sarla mocked. "The few left in this village", replies Meera. "Okay, you mean the 12 families remaining in Supela? The way people are dying every day, someday this village will be empty. Who will burn the last corpse? The more I think, the more I go insane", sighed Sarla.

The clouds have been rambling since the afternoon. The markets are closed. When Meera came to Supela after her marriage with Prabhat, she was 19. Initially, she never liked the village but within a few months, she started admiring its beauty. The greenery and the fresh fruits, not to forget the *melas*, the festivals, the evening snacks, Malti's *godh bharai*.. but everything has changed now. The pandemic has transformed the entire village.

Meera still recalls that dreadful day when she was new at Supela and didn't know the customs. Then she went to fetch water from the stream and the local women laughed at her because her *pallu* dropped from her forehead. She didn't bother to place it again. Kaamini *bua* told her that women must protect their chastity. A *pallu* indicates that the *bahu* is *gharelu* and *sanskari*. Later on, Kaamini *bua* herself was found sleeping with the sarpanch. Despite being a mother of five, how could she do such a thing? 46 isn't an age for romance and extramarital relations. Then, Meera was disgusted to hear this about *bua* but now, it's become a normal scenario for her. This village is full of such filthy veiled 'love' stories.

The downpour started as soon as Meera and Sarla reached home. 9-year-old Munni was supervising the rice in the oven. "Munni, again you've kept the onions close to the utensils, hey *Bhagwan*, now I have to wash those again", said Sarla. "Leave it *amma*, onions don't cause any harm, on top of that it's raining outside. Don't step out, you'll get drenched and catch a cold", said Meera. "Don't forget Meera, I'm a widow and so are you. We have to abide by certain rules, otherwise, society will corner us and we will go to hell after death."

"But these are all man-made rules amma, no God ever appeared on Earth and instructed the widows to survive on vegetables, then die of malnutrition. We all are God's child, God wouldn't wish to see us suffer", said Meera.

"You've read too many books, I'm telling you too much knowledge is dangerous for women", saying that Sarla took the utensils outside. When she returned with the utensils, she was drenched. That night, Sarla fell sick.

The next day Meera took her to the doctor's clinic. The doctor carefully observed Sarla, then recommended a RT-PCR test. The test results were positive. Sarla was covid positive. The doctor advised that she take the prescribed medicines, include animal protein in her diet, and stay isolated, but their house had only one room. Meera took the entire responsibility of her mother-in-law and asked Munni to sleep in the kitchen. For two weeks, Meera stayed with Sarla and served her like a trained nurse. While Sarla started to recover slowly, Meera fell sick. Sarla gave her *kadha* and some homemade medicines. The home remedies had little effect on ailing Meera. After two days, her condition worsened. She was having breathing problems. Munni and Sarla decided to call the doctor but the doctor refused to visit their home. He consulted over the phone and informed them that it was too late already. "Get her admitted to the city hospital", said the doctor.

The government hospital was almost 18 km from Supela. Before Sarla could gather help from the locals, Meera passed away leaving an orphan Munni. Munni was in deep shock, she witnessed how her mother suffered without proper attention, how she gasped during the last few hours, how she helplessly stared at Munni, how she stopped moving, how her eyes closed forever dropping a tear, how her body was wrapped in polythene bag and how the health workers threw it inside a van, just like garbage. Munni saw it all and could do nothing. Munni kept getting visions of that tragic day, repeatedly. She cried for several days and gradually, slipped into depression. Sarla was not sure what to do to make her beloved granddaughter smile again. Munni's health was deteriorating, she turned thinner than her age. Sarla, who never believed in medical science, now started to visit the doctor with Munni. After two visits, the doctor suggested that Sarla should take Munni to a psychiatrist. "Munni has lost appetite and she remains silent or asleep all day. Children of her age lead a super active lifestyle, they run, play, study, do household chores, but Munni is not doing any of those. It's alarming. If it continues for some more time, she will develop other chronic health conditions in addition to depression", said the doctor.

On the very first day of visiting the renowned psychiatrist Dr. Ridhi Dixit, Sarla was relieved. Munni uttered several sentences, she spoke to the doctor and answered her questions. The doctor skillfully managed to make Munni speak about what was troubling her. "I couldn't save my mother, she was my support system, my best friend, my guide, she was my inspiration, as she couldn't complete her studies, she wanted me to study and earn degrees. She was even saving money for my future. All my hope is gone now, I don't want to live the life of an ordinary village girl giving birth to a dozen kids. I don't have any purpose of staying alive now", Munni spoke her heart out at one go and broke down in tears. Dr. Dixit calmed her down, offered her a glass of water, wiped off her tears, and ensured that life wasn't going to be as bad as she thought it would. "That was enough for today, I will fix the next session after two weeks, meanwhile practice some meditation at home. Wait here, my assistant will show you the techniques and take the medicines regularly, that will work for the time being." Saying this, the doctor left. "Jai Siya Ram", Sarla exclaimed. She was determined to spend all her savings for the treatment of her only family member, alive.

The sessions with Dr. Dixit went pretty well for three months, but then Sarla was irritated. Dr. Dixit seemed too forward thinking, she simply nullified the concept of arranged marriage. "Live-in, that's necessary before marriage. You don't have to jump into a marriage because your grandmother wants you to get married or the society thinks it's time for you to get married. Do it on your terms, take your sweet time. Know your partner, stay together, and see if you can adjust with his negative traits. If all goes well, consider marrying them." That was her response when Munni told her that she was afraid of marriage.

"My mother got married at 19, I'm 9 already, I have higher studies to complete, I want to work in a reputed organization, but grandma often sulks as I'm a burden on her and she can't die without getting me married off", said Munni. "No worries Munni, the world has changed now, girls are getting equal opportunities. You just focus on your studies, excel, and keep in touch with me. I'll suggest some awesome scholarship programmes through which you can continue your education without being a burden on granny", assured Dr. Dixit. Since then, Sarla was pissed off with that doctor. "What kind of a doctor is she? She suggested Munni live-in with a stranger boy, chi chi.. She asked me to allow eggs and fish at home. Although she knows that…" Sarala decided to stop visiting her.

In a furious state of mind Sarla dialled Dr. Dixit, and informed her that she has been a bad influence for Munni, therefore, Sarala was going to discontinue the consultation. "Spending so much money just to buy some nonsensical ideologies is sheer luxury for poor people like us, doctor, I can't continue with this", said Sarla. "But Munni is coming out of the trauma, she needs someone who would listen to her without judgements. She has dreams to achieve Sarla, she's just 9 and has a long way to go. It's my duty as a doctor, to guide her and help her recover from the shock of

Meera's untimely demise. Please don't stop the session midway, I request you. I'm saying this for Munni's wellbeing", pleaded Dr. Dixit.

Two months later

Munni's health is much better now. She has started attending school again. Today, she will represent her school in a drama competition. Munni is extremely nervous about it. Before heading for a bath, she quickly rehearsed her lines. "Double, double toil and trouble; Fire burn, and cauldron bubble", as she uttered it, her grandmother came and hugged her from behind. "I didn't understand what you just said, but I understand that you love eggs and so I'm making it for lunch. Give your best performance and then together we will have *anda curry.*" Munni's anxious face turned happy in no time. The morale boost she got from the mere mention of egg curry was worth a watch.

Sarla doesn't know that Munni is still in touch with Dr. Dixit who taught her that being a widow is not a sin and getting married is not an achievement. The practices that Sarla have been following for years were actually laid down to suppress women, to keep them tied to norms, to deprive them from the pleasures of life, to keep them in control. Dr. Dixit opened Munni's eyes. Now, Munni often asks Sarla baffling questions, "Why do women wear *sindoor* and men don't?" Or "Why do widowed females wear white but widowed men don't have to wear a specific colour?" "These are all traditions, beta", that's all Sarla could respond. She could hardly find a logical explanation to Munni's abrupt queries.

During her hidden phone sessions with the doctor, Munni feels so enlightened. Dr. Dixit told her, "Don't let this social institution of marriage change your identity, food habits, dreams. Eat whatever you like, tell your grandmother to eat whatever she likes. Remember, there's no better cure than good food and sound sleep." Munni has successfully convinced Sarla to buy, cook, and eat eggs. Although she has not allowed meat yet, Munni knows dadi is her responsibility now and someday, she will take her to a Chinese eatery with her own earnings. Sarla was busy in the kitchen, when Munni came running, "Can I get a bite of the boiled egg *dadi*?" "Why are you so impatient? Let me cook the curry at least. The boiled egg is so bland," but Munni was in a hurry. "No, I'll eat the curry at lunch, for now just the boiled egg will do," saying that Munni grabbed her bottle. Sarala came quickly with a piece of boiled egg and put it in her mouth. Munni left. "*Aram se beta*," a concerned Sarala yelled, but Munni was gone far. Sarala looked at her way for sometime, then turned around, and walked inside the house. "Ting," some notification on Munni's phone showed up, Sarala saw a message from Dr. Dixit. She couldn't read it, but got tremendously angry. But as she clicked the home button, Meera's bright smiling face appeared.

Poem by Narita Ahuja

Angel at the Door!

One fine day A woman called the woman in me,
I heard from her, blurry voice, commendable was she,
As if i was day-dreaming my journey from new to old,
Felt everything around, so near and away, a story never told,
Before it ends, and leaves my picture in a frame,
Before it bends, I eagerly want to gain the respect, the fame.

A Daughter is always born on turmoil,
Disgracing the aspiration of a boy declared as royal,
By birth she's the goddess in all rituals,
but treated as a burden of worldly manuals,
Living, Learning, laughing, but in boundation,
Motherly gems act as an angel to her for foundations.

Daughter-in-law is only in name by law,
The angel now goes beyond her own,
She embraces and fulfils all, making them her own.
Gulping her dreams, satisfying everyone's expectations,

She learns and grows, feels and follows,
Tries to do her best, yet her feelings she never shows.

Wife is not just woman without life,
But a life through companionship to thrive,
Adding colours in her days, his nights,
Love, care, warmth, in between all tiffs and flights,
Angel is the understanding between the two,
Make it a bond forever to abide through,

To be a mother, is to be on cloud nine,
Soon the Angel will have her own sunshine,
Everything seemed to be so flawless,
She just thanked the beautiful goddess.
Gratitude was the angel for the moment she thought,
But a thunderstorm awaited her, she had no clue what not.

And the lines started bleeding in posthaste,
She held and screamed and pleaded to wait.
But it won't listen, affrighted she called her man.
Shattering her dream forever,
Devastating her heart out like never.
No source of light, No hope to shine,
Mere dim humdrum, with none of her own.

Here I shared a story of a girl having angelic miles,
Being a daughter, daughter-in-law, and a wife,
Though it's a journey of every women I see,
Every mother,
Every sister,
Every friend,
Every colleague,
Life at every stage is full of struggles,
Tremendous ups and downs with juggles,
As this cruel world never lets them sleep,
Complaints and compromises they never tell,
Moved on to what everyone desired from them,
Killed their aim, their dreams for familia which less loved them,
Philosophically graded in upward appreciations,
Physically deteriorated in many dimensions,
Still Accepting and adoring life as it comes,
Seizing the day and locking the nights for whatever remains,

Seeking happiness in everyone's smile,
Walking all alone, nobody by her side,
All of them need her presence,
but never asked in her absence,
Her silence is always taken as a myth,
But has all the voice to say to say the truth,

She gave her heart and soul to her universe,
Silently awaited her day to be vice-verse.

That night was full of treasure,
I wanted to forget all my pains in pleasure,
The more I believe everything is according to lord's will,
Surrendering was the only source until,
An Angel came to visit me,
Wearing pious clothes, a supreme soul,
Beauty glorified, power exemplified,
Spreading the light of auspicious aura,
Came near me and ask,
Never feel disheartened, it will not last,
Believe in your lord, anchor your life,
I started crying for all my miseries,
She held me tight,
Hugged all the while,
She was contagious in her vibes,
Goosebumps to me and everyone in the tribe,
She glared at me from the corner of room,
I was quietly acknowledging her fading away all my doom.

That angel was an incarnation of Shakti on earth,

As shared by lord Krishna to his parth,
She visited me to glorify my reason of birth,
All genders have divinity,
No more, no less, virtue is equanimity,
If Women can be amplified creator,
Then she can a dangerous destroyer,
Recognising her persona is the matter of fact,
This 21st century is all for empower, enrich and enact.

She graced me with her continuous eyes,
Sharing a deep embarking journey in her smile,
Hold my hand if you wish to live a life,
Where people will cry when you die,
Expressed her emotions in very few words,
To make me understand what was not said or heard,
Her true passion was to serve others always,
Make this world a blissfully blessed human race.

She was my lesson for life to live it large all while,
How to Balance work-life with all the smiles,
I, the woman, want to empower you every day,
Hassle free life should be your ambition each day,
As People will love you twice in sayings:
when you are giving &
when you expect nothing,
You yourself are a divine angel in every aspect,

Fulfilling responsibilities, learning from every reject,
Be thankful for the lord showering you the best,
It's his planning, handling everything for best.
The angel left me with God's knowledge,
Realising my existence to acknowledge,
Restarted my journey as a woman,
Supporting each woman in my clan,
Establishing me as a homemaker, teacher,
and now an entrepreneur.
And it was a dream come true,
Holding my productions in my hands,
My twins babies: one girl and my enterprise,
Today I feel complete, journey of a woman into a mom,
and from a homemaker to a management head.

It is my journey of struggle, sustain, and conquest,
Turn down the honkers who feel you are a mess,
Stop living life just for others,
Self-care is a necessity, not leisure.
They will say, You are selfish but do not give it a thought,
Earn the coins and courage which you always forget.
Merge the diva and divine in you,
To wear your crown of queen and be happy be you.

Short Story by
Dr. Barnali Das

The Cage

The female gaze…

It's an infinite expansion of the cage.

She sees the circle of life unleashing her eternal dance.

She stares at the world, perplexed, numb!
Is she in a trance?
She is submerged in tonight's deadly calm.

Life flies by, and it's easy to get lost in the blur. Dr. Anita Chugh in greyish blue linen sari, loose braid, fine lines of grey eye liner and light brown lipstick is personification of grace. Once you see her, the personality keeps an impression in the mind. Ani is engrossed in the file of bed number three of ICU of GTB Hospital. She is feeling a little uneasy. The resident doctors and staff nurse are following her.

Parul, a housewife in her forties and mother of two children, stares at them blankly in a daze, battling with her pain and mental agony. Suddenly the sharp alarm of saturation drop startles everyone. Ani touches Parul's wounded hands. Parul is kept in a prone position with PD catheters emerging from her belly, like something from a Michael Crichton novel. The incident took place at 7 pm yesterday. Just before the turn of the neighborhood - the strong hand of the rapist snatched everything from Parul's world. Parul can still faintly remember two or three half-familiar faces, covered with black masks.

Dr. Anita is still disturbed by quarrels over the morning breakfast table. This time again a single line in the pregnancy test kit brings turmoil in her well settled life. The intensity of Ramen's glare and the sarcasm of the mother-in-law's voice are still crushing her mind and soul. The hope of this few days of the month is now again submerged in the pull of despair.

Ani can still remember the loving, soft spoken and cultured Ramen, her MBBS buddy and now her husband. And today! Ani is daily abused by Ramen mentally, and sometimes he raises his hands too. Ahh! Ani is tired and wounded. Her self-reflection throws light on the ostracization and victimization faced by Parul, Ani and many other women in the society. Ani can relate to the feelings and sense of imprisonment of women.

Grr Grrrr Grrrrr - Suddenly Ani delved into the sordid realities of surroundings. The nurse is aspirating fluids from Parul's rhyles tube. The female rape victim in the ICU's bed number three and the medicine conslutant! Parul's vulnerability makes Ani more tormented. Ani responds to her patient with the same honesty, the same vulnerability. The vulnerability of women is visible from the fact that they are living in an unseen cage. Ani wants to experience a sense of closure.

Staring into the crimson-red rising sun,
She sees the circle of life unleashing its eternal dance.
She stares at it, perplexed, numb!
Is she in a trance?
'Coz she keeps running around life's circle.
Hoping to catch life's profound miracle,
Of how tomorrow's life exposure-
Transforms tonight's deadly calm into a new closure.

Poem by Bhawna Mishra

I am Woman

I am today's woman

I am not less than man

Although I have to prove it

"Weak" that tag hard to remove it

Life is hard for us

Do you believe it?

No I am struggling day & night

Still I have to fight for it

Balancing home and office

When nobody notice

What is our real motif?

What is my real worth?

Searching my identity

Why & whom to prove my chastity

Fighting for gender equality

Yes I am modern woman

I am not less than man

Although we touched moon

But can't decide lunch for noon

Why she needs permission

Remains always in hesitation

But I am today's woman.

Short Story by Debanjali Nag

Bitter & Beautiful

Little Neha was growing up with the love and upbringing of her mother. Neha's papa was a moody arrogant government office senior officer and her mother was a college teacher.

Neha was very much in love with her mother. When she grew up a little, she became like her mother of a good nature.

Her father always used to punish her because she was weak in studies. Neha wanted to be a teacher like her mother. In school, she used to participate mostly in painting and dance and used to come first. She had another talent in art and craft. When she was in class 5, everyone took pride in the writing competition of the school. The story and poetry written by her touched everyone's mind and made her happy.

As soon as the results of class 12 exams came, Neha begged her father to give her a chance, to study her favorite subject. Neha's father was a stubborn person.

Enrolled in commerce Neha waited for when she would finish her graduation. Finally passed B.Com and that too with such low rank. Neha's father used to say that Neha should try for a government job. Neha took that path and even went back. She liked poetry and story. The passion to become a writer was fizzing in her head.

One day Neha's closest friend explained that she studied more first so that she could also do her favorite job. After a few exams got admission in MB, Neha used to study hard. Meanwhile, a boy came into her life and whom she mistook as an angel, he was mean like a demon and her college friend was engaged in making her life hell by collaborating with the same boy.

Still, Neha did not fall weak, her teachers gave her full support. Whatever difficulties she had been facing in her life made her a brave girl.

In college, when her teachers came to know about her writing, they sent her to participate in the inter-college fests, even she went on to win. She finished her studies, then got a job, but her father did not allow her to do the job. Neha was all grown up as per him now, worthy of marriage. Neha never agreed that she should marry and have children and this should be her life.

Neha's mother stayed by her side. One fine day she got a good job. Not even a year passed and some people in her office became her enemies. Neha's manager and seniors loved her poetry as well her nature. These things used to knock in the eyes of some people. During the job, Neha fell in love with a boy in her office and that boy was pretending to be in love with her. That boy needed a trophy girlfriend to show the world. But when Neha came to know about the truth, she lost her faith in love. Neha took the decision to leave the job, and this time her father refused to do so because they thought that may be Neha's job will help her get a good boy and it will be easy for her to get married. Neha's dream was not suppressed, she kept trying every day everywhere, how she went ahead to fulfill her dreams. Meanwhile, a friend of her gave a writing job for his business. Neha had even given it in writing, but she did not know that this work of hers would give her more courage to move forward.

Then gradually she started receiving work from all sources. She kept on writing. Not only Hindi, but also used to write poetry in English, which some foreign writers liked on social media. She kept getting more work but Neha was not happy. She wanted to go to Mumbai because it was the only place where her dreams could come true. Neha had to leave her family.

Till now 2 friends of her school kept giving her courage and stood by her so that she does not fall weak mentally. And the family members of both of them also loved Neha equally. When Neha left for Mumbai, the family members of both of her friends kept giving courage to Neha's mother. Here Neha was struggling everyday in Mumbai for her work to talk to a big director or producer. But Neha was spending her days doing petty things. Ritusree was working in another city, stayed away from her family in Bangalore. She used to go to Mumbai to meet Neha sometimes. Her life was also not easy.

Ritusree was a middle class girl and her family members raised her with a lot of love and care. Ritusree tried hard to fulfill her dreams. She wanted to become a teacher, but she was doing a good job in an MNC. She had Deep in her life and he was also her childhood friend, working with her in Bangalore. Neha's life was going through difficulties anyway. She used to miss her mother everyday but she chose her career, so she had to leave her family according to her father's condition. A happy moment came in Neha's life during her struggle days but Neha was oblivious. Neha's work was loved by a musician, her simplicity, her efforts captured his heart.

He did not want to help Neha by pity, he was also a boy with principles. Seeing Neha's passion towards her work, he gave her an opportunity to write a song for a film. Both Ritusree and Deep together were giving financial support to Neha during her struggling days. Neha was grateful to both of Ritusree and Deep for all their love and support. Ritusree was looking for a boy for her friend Neha, who is a true and good person. Deep came to know that Neha likes the musician and he got scared what if again she gets cheated. Before speaking to Ritusree, Deep thought of talking to Rohit. Rohit admitted that he is a divorcee but he truly loved her with all his heart. He told Deep as soon as a girl like Neha came into his life, his sorrows subsided. He too was cheated by his first wife. Neha's goodness made Rohit believe in love again. Couldn't keep an eye on Rohit, Deep asked his friend who was in Mumbai to find out about Rohit. Rohit's one bitter truth came out that during his college time, he had killed a boy to save the life of a girl so much that Rohit had to go to jail. As soon as he came to know about this, Deep talked to Ritusree. Ritusree then explained to Deep that for a few more months, Rohit should be observed. How does he behave with other people and how does he treat Neha.

Neha's career was growing rapidly. One after the other, she got work. Sometimes people used to cheat Neha with her earnings by giving less money in return for her hard work. Neha's first wish was to find a true life partner, she was lost somewhere but at that time Rohit supported her. He was doing this for the happiness of Neha, even brought her mother to Mumbai, kept it at his house. Neha was unaware of it.

One day Rohit took Neha to meet someone in connection with a work and there she met her mother. After years, the mother daughter were seeing each other. They could not could not control themselves and cried hugging each other. Ritusree called Rohit at the same time and luckily Rohit picked up the phone and gave it to Neha's mother. When Neha's mother told about Rohit, Deep and Ritusree decided to go to Mumbai. There was not only Neha's mother in Mumbai. There was also Ritusree's mother whom Neha and Rohit had brought to the meet. Rohit tried to get Ritusree and Deep married with the blessings of her mother. Then the opportunity came to bring Neha's father to Mumbai. Ritusree and Simmi's mother and father got together to bring Neha's father to Mumbai. Ritusree, Simmi, Neha's friendship was deep rooted. Rohit's nobility had kissed everyone's heart. Neha's father decided that she should get married soon to Rohit. But Neha did not want to get married. Rohit was just a good friend to Neha. Neha used to share all her happiness and sorrows with him.

Rohit was not able to tell what were his feelings for Neha. Marriage was a deal for Neha, she decided to marry a boy who would be a husband for the namesake. Rohit still kept her career ahead for the happiness of Neha, and started searching a guy for her. Neha's father was no longer the same as before, he used to like Rohit very much for his daughter. Ritusree tried to explain Neha that her thinking was wrong in her mind but Neha was only in love with her work. She was determined. She didn't want to think about anything else at that moment. Rohit had lost his parents long ago in an accident. He grew up with his sister at his aunt's house and she was their guardian since then. He belonged from a wealthy family. His nature and humane nature with a big heart and humbleness made differentiated him from many other rich guys. Life snatched away the happiness at a tender age and eventually pushed him through much hardships emotionally which broke him from inside. Still, for once, he did not utter a single word to Neha about his feelings for her.

The search was on for the boy. For Neha, he found a suitable boy and fixed their wedding which did not make anyone happy. A strange and painful thing happened to Neha on her wedding day. The groom who was about to get married with Neha had run away in the middle of the rituals at his home. His parents could not trace him and had to call off the wedding. This news could have affected her terribly and all of Neha's friends and family along with Rohit was suppressed.

Rohit did not let Neha know. Both the families of Rohit and Neha along with their friends decided to send Rohit to marry Neha. They were scared though had no choice and had to think of Neha. This time she would have broken and ended all her faith in people. After getting married, Neha came to know that Rohit is her husband and not the real groom. Neha misunderstood Rohit. To this added another shock to Neha when she found Ritusree and Simmi standing by Rohit's side. She could not imagine and was clueless about everything. She could hardly believe her eyes as well her fate. Everyone tried making Neha understand that Rohit saved her honour. The groom had left even before coming to the wedding ceremony. This piece of news broke her from within and she could not bear the bitter truth of her fate mocking at her everytime in each and every single relationship. She felt so disgusted and helpless. Neha's friends tried making her understand how she was betrayed by a stranger but Rohit did not leave her for her dignity and respects her. They all pleaded her to give him a chance to prove his love for her. As days passed, gradually the distance between Neha and Rohit started fading off. After few months, Rohit's family were looking for a guy to get his sister married. Neha took all the initiative and did everything to search an apt person for her sister-in-law. She was all lovey dubby in her marriage and tried to keep everyone happy in her family. Rohit's aunt brought the information about the men who were eligible for Rohit's sister.

A day was fixed for the meeting with the groom's family. Neha had prepared her sister-in-law beautifully and brought in front of everyone. While introducing her with the groom's family, Neha looked at him and was in utter shock. It was the same person who left Neha before marrying her. The guy felt uncomfortable and stayed silent. She went to take Rohit in the kitchen and told about the groom. Rohit called the police without a second thought and this time got the guy arrested.

Rohit finally got the support of Neha as his life partner and also in his work.

About the Authors

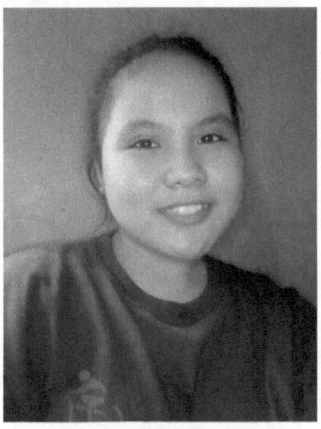

Khrystine Soldao

Khrystine Soldao is an eleventh-grade student. Reading is just one of her hobbies but writing is her passion. She doesn't have enough courage to speak what's on her mind. So, she writes it instead. She has too many flaws but that is not enough for her to give up on her dreams. Besides that, watching dramas, listening to music, and playing online games are her hobbies as well. And one fun fact about her is when she's too stressed out because of the school loads, screaming and singing out of tune is her reliever.

Isha Chopra

Isha Chopra graduated from Delhi University and post-graduated from Ignou University. She's simple, sorted, enthusiastic and keen in learning new things. She's fun loving, adventurous, creative, passionate, talented, loves to spread positivity, all-rounder and much more. She has been a part of many anthologies along with one international anthology. She has been a part of many writing contests and won some of them at great ranks. She was recently honored with the "Literature Star of the Year" award in 2021. In her words: "Be someone's sunshine, there's a lot of critics already. Be the light in someone's heart, which can give you immense happiness."

Piyali Mitra

Piyali loves giving color to her imagination through words. She enjoys writing poetries of things happening around her. She draws inspiration from the daily activities and characters unfolding before her. Piyali's passion for poetry led to publish a solo book on poetry, Of the Heart and Soul: A Mellifluous Whisper, and also contribute to various volumes of poetry. She has been part of the Ukiyoto Publisihng project My Heart Goes On, of which the book Words Unsaid has been recently published as part of the project. She has received various awards and prizes for poetry writing both at her home country and from abroad.

Sudakshina Bhatta

Sudakshina, better known by her pseudonym Rottenheart, is an aspiring author who has a knack for creative and business writing. She completed her MBA in marketing but didn't choose to be a marketing professional. Instead, she decided to follow her passion for writing and become a full time writer. Presently, she's working on her upcoming novel which will be completed by 2022. When she's not writing, she is most probably brainstorming about a topic to write next. Sudakshina is a huge Bollywood buff. Gulzar's lyrics, Rahman's music, Mani Ratnam's direction, are some of the ingredients of Bollywood that inspire her to think differently. She finds solace in Ruskin Bond's stories. She is a part-time comedian who makes herself happy by spreading laughter among her family, friends and acquaintances. Read her quotes on her Instagram page Mousy Madhatter.

Narita Ahuja

Writing makes her more of herself! Narita is a Japanese word which means to be inventive. Professionally She is a lecturer in Commerce and as an explorer, she has ventured into academics and photography professionally, and added to her avocations contemporary dancing, clay modeling, designing and creative writing. As a blogger and a writer, she intends to explore the parallel world of words and take her readers on new adventures of life, through her 15 books co-authored, including international publication. She successfully completed a masterclass in creative writing and the UNLU creative writing course by Ruskin Bond. She was awarded the "Most Influential person 2021" by Cherry Book Awards. She has started a new venture as a co-founder of "am_power" to empower everyone around through her expertise.

Follow her on:
Facebook: NARITART
Instagram: naritaart_ and _am_power

Dr. Barnali Das

Dr Barnali Das has come a long way but she is still so full of dreams and aspirations for the future. She is MD, DNB and consultant in Laboratory Medicine. She has been honored as "Best Docs Mumbai" in 2020, 2021 and 2022 in the magazine Outlook and India Today's "Top Doctors Mumbai, 2020 & 2021." Dr. Barnali is recipient of many national & international awards for her scientific work. Her biography has been featured in a book named And So Can You (where 17 successful doctors share their inspiring stories). She has many international and national scientific publications and her interview and mention of her work have been published in magazines & newspapers, like Times of India, Hindustan Times, Dainik Jagran etc. She philosophizes a lot. Dr. Barnali received the Sambad Sahitya Award. She has also authored a book, A Aa Ka Kha r Mela, Charay Chobite Khela, which was released at the Kolkata Book Fair, in 1999. Still she writes poems, short stories and articles for newspapers and magazines

Bhawna Mishra

Bhawna Mishra is a research scholar in the P.G Department of English of Magadh University, Bodh Gaya, Bihar. She is the co-author of more than 22 anthologies. Her own anthology is under publication. She is also the assistant editor of Satrachee, an International bilingual journal. She is equally active in Hindi literature too, her poems and stories have been published in Hindustan Patna edition. She has presented her research papers in both National & international seminars. She has received INSC awards for her research paper in 2020. She was awarded in March 2021 by Herstory Times, for her active participation in "Prithvi," a women climate warrior campaign.

Debanjali Nag

Debanjali, an author and a corporate job holder, balances her professional life with a lot of twists and turns. Writing helps her express her emotions and motivates to increase her creative imagination. At the same time, she loves to paint and give a touch of vividness to her imaginative characters on the oil canvas. Hailing from the city of joy, settling in Bengaluru for her job keeps her on toes but she never fails to miss the opportunity to vibe with the creative meetings with the authors and painters across the country.

www.ingramcontent.com/pod-product-compliance
Lightning Source LLC
LaVergne TN
LVHW041547070526
838199LV00046B/1861